JAN BRETT

THE UMBRELLA

G. P. PUTNAM'S SONS • NEW YORK

Published simultaneously in Canada.
Manufactured in China by South China Printing Co. Ltd.
Designed by Gunta Alexander. Text set in Badger Medium.
The art was done in watercolors and gouache.
Airbrush backgrounds by Joseph Hearne.

Library of Congress Cataloging-in-Publication Data
Brett, Jan, 1949–   The umbrella / Jan Brett.   p.   cm.
Summary: Carlos goes into the cloud forest to look for
animals, but he manages to miss seeing them even
though they have an adventure with his umbrella.
[1. Rain forest animals—Fiction. 2. Umbrellas—Fiction.]
I. Title.   PZ7.B75225Umb 2004   [E]—dc22   2003027853
ISBN 978-0-399-24215-1

10 9 8 7 6   First Impression

With special thanks to
Nicole Brocco and Lois Ostapczuk

For
Bethany
Susana
Fusiek

"Hey, little Carlos, where are you going with that umbrella?"

"Into the cloud forest, Papa, to see what I can see. I'll be spotting a jaguar and a monkey. For sure I'll spy a toucan and a kinkajou. I'll keep my eyes peeled for a shy tapir."

"*Buena suerte*, Carlos, good luck," Papa says.

Carlos walks into the cloud forest. How silent it is. The only sound is the drip, drip, drip of drops falling from the tall trees.

There's not so much as a tiny tree frog down here, Carlos thinks. I'll have to climb up for a better view.

Carlos drops his umbrella and starts up the giant fig tree.

Drip, drip, drip. A little puddle appears in the green umbrella.

A tiny tree frog leaps down and slips into the water. *"Hola,"* Froggy croaks happily. "I have this puddle all to myself." He sinks down until only his eyes peep out.

Plop! A juicy, ripe fig falls smack into the umbrella. Toucan is not far behind.

Froggy sees Toucan's sharp beak. *"¡Vete!"* he peeps. "Go away!" But Toucan is not moving, he's waiting for another fig to fall.

High in the tree, a scratching sound starts. Scratch . . .
scratch . . . SCRATCH! Something is sliding down the tree.
It gets louder and louder until THUMP — Kinkajou tumbles in.
"*¡Muy grande!*" Froggy squeaks. "You're too big!"
"You can't stay here!" Toucan says.
But Kinkajou is just getting comfortable. After prowling
around all night for food, he's found just the right place to rest.

Thump! Crash! Thump! Baby Tapir blunders into the
green umbrella. "Blaaht, blaaaaaaht!" he bawls. "Mama!"

"*¡No está aquí! She's not here!*" Froggy shouts, along
with hungry Toucan and sleepy Kinkajou.

The umbrella's shiny green leaves shiver and shake, but
Baby Tapir is staying here until his mother comes for him.

Swish! Swish! A most beautiful bird sails down onto
the umbrella handle. Quetzal looks down at Froggy, Toucan,
Kinkajou and Baby Tapir, rocking back and forth.
"Fly away," they call up. But proud Quetzal is too
busy arranging his tail plumes to listen to them.

Suddenly, frisky Monkey jumps down. He grabs the umbrella, flings it into the river and jumps aboard.

"*¿Qué pasa?* What is happening?" Froggy asks as water starts to pour into the umbrella.

"We will sink for sure!" Toucan, Kinkajou, Baby Tapir and Quetzal wail together. "That Monkey never thinks before he acts."

"¡*Atención!* Who's sitting on me?" Froggy cries.

"Stop poking your beak into me," Kinkajou shouts at Toucan.

"Blaaht!" bawls Baby Tapir.

"You're getting my feathers all wet," Quetzal squawks at Monkey.

Jaguar is cleaning his silky black spots when he hears all the squabbling and looks up.

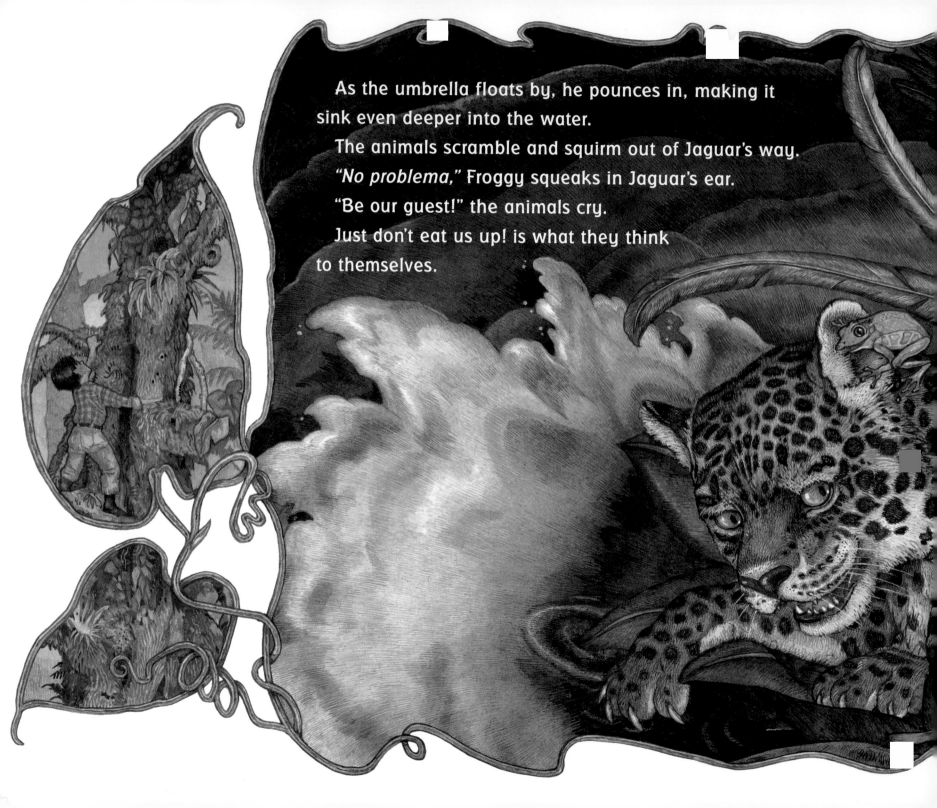

As the umbrella floats by, he pounces in, making it
sink even deeper into the water.
The animals scramble and squirm out of Jaguar's way.
"No problema," Froggy squeaks in Jaguar's ear.
"Be our guest!" the animals cry.
Just don't eat us up! is what they think
to themselves.

Hummingbird flashes by, smaller than small.
He sees the big green umbrella handle sticking up,
just the place for a hummingbird to stop for a little rest.
　As he is about to land, they all start shouting.
"No room," big boy Jaguar snarls.
"Move on," Monkey hollers.
"Find another place," Quetzal sings out.
"We got here first," Kinkajou growls.
"Stay away," Toucan screeches.
"Blaaaht," bawls Baby Tapir.
"¡Adiós! Good-bye!" Froggy peeps.
But Hummingbird lands anyway.

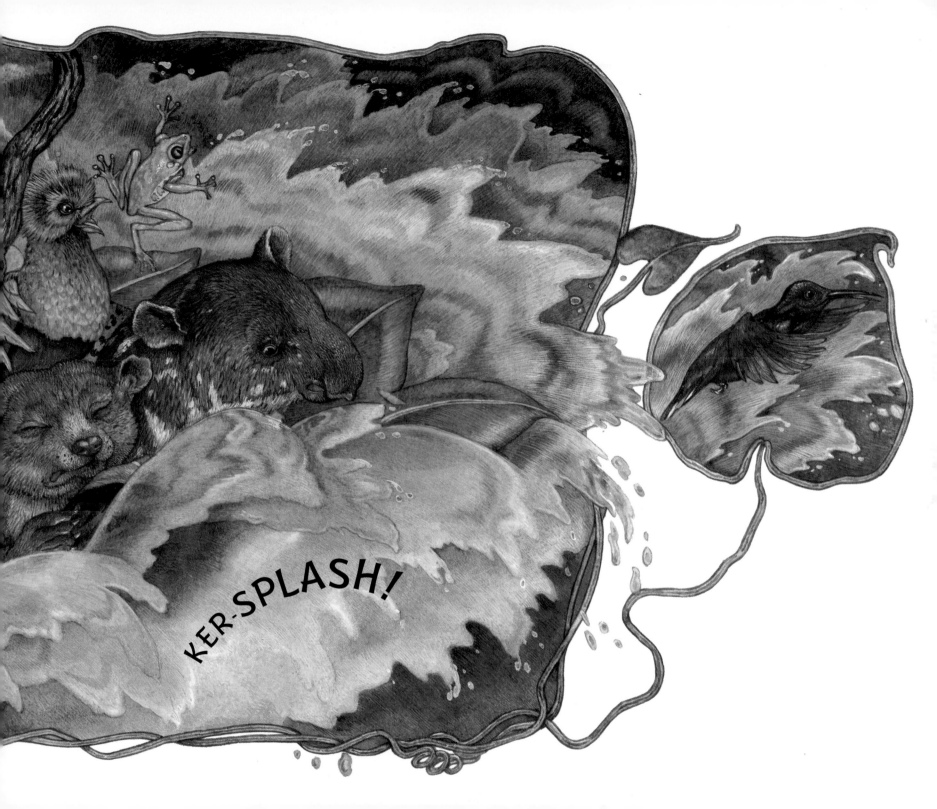

KER-SPLASH!

The umbrella tumbles over, and everyone falls out.
Jaguar, Quetzal, Baby Tapir, Kinkajou, Toucan, Monkey
and Froggy all clamber up the bank as the umbrella pops
to the surface and drifts back to shore.

Up in the giant fig tree, Carlos looks out at the sea of green.
"No animals today," he sighs. "I wonder where they all are."
He climbs down, picks up his umbrella and walks toward home.

The sun shines through the green leaves
of the umbrella, and Carlos sees the silhouette of
the tiny tree frog.

"Hey, little froggy, try hitchhiking with me
tomorrow, and I'll show you a real adventure.
I'm going back to the cloud forest to find a toucan,
a kinkajou, maybe even a monkey or a shy tapir.
I bet I'll see a jaguar too. And I'm going to find
that quetzal for sure."

Carlos props the umbrella outside his door. Drip, drip, drip. Water falls from the roof. A little puddle appears in the green umbrella. Froggy slides down the handle and slips into the water.

"*¡Hola!*" Froggy splashes happily. "I have this puddle all to myself."